Little Roo liked fun,
so she sneaked a peek at them.
"Would you like to play, too?"
asked Mummy Kangaroo.
"No," said Little Roo. "I only like
playing in Mummy's pocket."

GUIDO VAN GENECHTEN

Little
Roo
and the
Big Wide World

ALISON GREEN BOOKS

Mummy Kangaroo was getting very tired of carrying Little Roo.

"You're too big for Mummy's pocket now," she said.

"Wouldn't you like to hop around by yourself?"

"I wouldn't like that at all," said Little Roo.

"I like it in Mummy's pocket."

"Mummy's pocket is the
best place in the world," said Little Roo.
"How do you know?" asked Mummy Kangaroo.
"The world is big and wide,
and all you've seen is my pocket."
"I just know," said Little Roo.

"Hoppity-hoppity-hoppity," sang Little Roo,
as Mummy hopped on through the jungle.
"Look at the monkeys," said Mummy, "swinging through
the trees! Aren't they clever? Would you like to play with them?"
Little Roo sat up. They were clever. But it all looked a bit scary.
"I think it's safer in Mummy's pocket," she said at last.

"Hoppity-hoppity-hoppity!" shouted Little Roo, and she bounced up and down in her mummy's pocket. Soon they came to a wide open plain. "**Look!**" said Little Roo. "Giraffes! Aren't they running fast, Mummy!"

"Ever so fast," said Mummy Kangaroo.
"Would you like to run with them?"
"Oh, no," said Little Roo. "They're running far too
far away from Mummy's pocket."